First U.S. edition 1997.
Printed in China. Published
in the United States by
Little Friend Press,
Scituate, Massachusetts.

ISBN: 1-890453-01-3

Library of Congress Catalog
Card Number: 97-071679

To Kelly,
1-4-3

LITTLE FRIEND PRESS
28 NEW DRIFTWAY
SCITUATE, MASSACHUSETTS 02066

The Wishing Star

Written and illustrated by
Diane R. Houghton

LITTLE FRIEND PRESS

SCITUATE, MASSACHUSETTS

Emily looked up at the sky.

A shining shimmer caught her eye.

A speckle with a twinkling tail,

That left a golden glitter trail.

She saw the object hit the ground,

With gold dust bursting all around.

She woke her little brother Dan,

And to the garden gate they ran.

What they saw was quite a surprise.

It made them blink and rub their eyes.

"How lucky the two of us are...

For we have found a wishing star!"

A special star it was it's true,

Of such a brilliant golden hue.

As they ran over to their find,

The star began to speak its mind.

"Hurray!" the star said with delight.

"I'm glad you found me on this night.

Please get me back up to the sky.

I'll grant you a wish if you'll try."

"A wish for us?" they asked with glee.

"What will we wish for...oh let's see."

"This choice will be so hard indeed."

"What do we want...what do we need?"

"A mermaid's what I'd like to be,

Frolicking in a deep blue sea!

That's what I want to be my wish,

To swim in water like a fish!"

Dan stood and thought without a word,

Then said, "I'd like to be a bird!

I'd soar above the Earth so high.

It would be so much fun to fly!"

"You need to hurry," the star frowned.

"For soon I will not be around.

My powers will begin to wane,

Until I'm in the sky again."

"Let's use our wish to send him home,

So he won't be here all alone."

The pair then shut their eyes so tight.

And sent this wish out to the night.

"We wish that we could find a way
To save the star we found today."
Stars are just like children you see.
Home is where we all want to be.

Emily and Dan looked around.
They saw a basket on the ground.
Struggling to lift its stubborn top,
A huge balloon burst open...Pop!

They grabbed the star and hopped inside,

Ready for an exciting ride!

They rose so high to see the view,

Of land so vast and sea so blue.

Then suddenly, they saw a hook.

"Let's sail over and take a look."

The star gave out a happy yell.

"That's the same spot from which I fell!"

As they returned him to his place,

A shining smile lit up his face.

He said, "I'll give you one last try

To wish before we say good-bye."

"The only wish we have right now,

Is if there's some way you know how,

To let us know that you're OK,

At the finish of every day."

"Each night before you go to sleep,

Here is a promise I will keep...

Just look up to this very place,

So I can see your smiling face."

"Then I will twinkle 1-4-3.

That's a sign for you both from me,

Since 1-4-3 means I love you,

And you have made my wish come true."

The balloon began to descend.

Their adventure was at the end.

They knew that their unselfish deed

Had helped a new found friend in need.

Each night before they go to sleep,

Out of their comfy beds they leap.

They search high up into the air,

To see if that star is still there.

He twinkles what they hope to see,

One twinkle, four twinkles, then three.

They know he sees them for it's true,

That 1-4-3 means I love you.

E
HOU
(TOD)

Houghton, Diane R.
The wishing star /

9/28/09

14.95
REN.

6/12/02